OF BLOOD AND BATTLE

A FANTASY STORY

JONATHAN EVAN HUDSON

OF BLOOD AND BATTLE

JACOB PRAY

In his precious amber wool habit, Jacob Pray slipped up the spiral of small stone steps as if nothing was unusual, as if the utter silence below was normal, rather than the usual hymns and choirs chanting prayers to the one and only god of all, the Lightful One, for another day of grace and beauty.

The pine railing to the side was as sturdy as always. His hand rested on it, sliding along the round railing, supporting his march like the Lightful One had supported Jacob himself.

Even when Jacob hadn't been worthy of the support.

There were a total of three hundred and fifty two steps up the chapel tower , exactly, and one of three chapel towers here in Saphold City.

Two more than most towns and cities throughout the land of Athedia.

All the steps were cut unevenly but not a single one was wobbly. Never wobbly. Ever.

For that would suggest a wobbling sense of faith, of skepticism toward the Lightful One, and no monk of the Grand Order of the Lightful One would ever dare be skeptic and wear the precious amber habit.

His big hands held the thick tome of his faith. It was a heavy weight, but his sin was even heavier, from the many deaths by his own big hands. Human deaths. This solitary life of religious duty was now his only hope of salvation. Ringing the giant church bells of solid bronze each day at the designated times, his calling. All thanks to this Tome of the Lightful One. Its cover of bleached white leather was like the shield his own faith granted him.

Of the protection of the faithful by the Lightful One.

That the faintest hint of blood now reached his sensitive nose, through his thick white beard, no, the quiet tap-tap-tap of heavy boots, all following him up the spiral stair, but slowly, steadily, careful not to reveal their presence—yet.

Now he knew why he lived while so many had died, even by his own hands, no less.

Today was the day.

He must reach the church bells. Ring a warning of an attack.

Warn all of Saphold City their days of peace were at an end. That their foolish festival today, the so-called Festival of Flame and Passion, would soon end in utter disaster.

For the stink of wolf, of tiger, even of fox ... a bestial stink mixed strongly with the regular sweaty smells of humanity ...

the quietest of grunts, of growls, of mews ... all coming from the spiraling stairway below him.

Jacob dared not show a single hint of hurrying—yet.

For in his previous life, during his sinful times, he had actually fought beside such creatures, such monsters as one of their many barbaric human allies. Monster or human, all were all-too-awe-struck by their all-power, all-invincible dragon overlords. Each breed of those monsters, known generally as beastmites, all had a build similar enough to a human's.

But unlike real genuine humans, they had features of that beast as well. A short fur coat. Big bestial ears from the top sides of their head. A tail from the nap of their back. Pawish hands and feet.

Most obvious of all—despite their human-shaped head and face they had a snout or maw instead of a human mouth and nose.

Worst of all some beastmites could shift into a completely human form and then back their true beastmite form.

But those vile monsters didn't realize just how many steps were here between Jacob and the end of this spiral stairway.

Or between him and them.

First would be the wolfmites. Big in brawn and battle lust. All too eager to tear down their prey. Their muscular bodies were so strong, so tough neither ordinary steel nor mundane magic posed much of a threat to them.

Then would be the tigermites.

Eager to toy with any who dared survive the wolfmites.

Not as strong, or as tough as wolfmites, but the males were still far stronger than humans. Both males and females far faster in speed. And able to hide in shadow. Some could even jump between shadows.

Shadowjumping it was called.

Then the sneaky foxmites and their fell elemental magicks. All in all they were far less tough than even a tiger-mite. Hinds less protective but their healing was far too good. They could even regrow lost limbs, as long as their stamina lasted, and they weren't staked through the heart.

Worst of all even the weakest foxmites could create and command some kind of flame.

Stronger foxmites could even become flame. Wicked living sentient flame.

So Jacob and his big strong hands might delay the wolfmites, but only for a few moments. A squad of beastmites always consisted of three to thirteen and—

The howl of a wolf. No. A wolfmite embracing his inner wicked wolf.

"For the Revolution! For the All Powerful Manticore Lord rules all!"

The leader of the squad no doubt. Kill him and the second-in-command, the beastmite squad would lose its leadership, its focus on its objective.

Jacob almost turned around.

But no.

Several other wolfmite howls followed the first.

"Death to the weak! Death to mankind! Death to the Chosen Ones!!!"

Chosen Ones?

His heart sank quicker than any stone. His feet moved faster and faster.

For the Chosen Ones were the mankind's only hope to find and defeat the greatest evil in all of Athedia, the Darkest One, once again, in whatever form that shapeshifting being of great evil took this eon.

More vicious howls erupted from below.

No need to look down. Give those monsters any encouragement. Any satisfaction at the bloodshed Jacob would see below, at the bottom, and the heartache he'd feel for not fighting, dying with all the others.

No doubt now. The Lightful Ones rarely left room for the faithful to truly doubt.

He launched into a run.

Until the wicked gruff voice of something worse than any beastmite—a ratling—a monster as big and brutally powerful as a troll—a deformed man-like brute thrice the height of the tallest man and twice the girth and in pure brawn—but with the features and fury of a big black rat.

The ratling growled the utterly unexpected from the very bottom of the stairway.

"Snow," the ratling said. "Some flame. *Now.* Or else Greenstead Village and your precious Maverick de Mayhem are *next.*"

Then a loud gagging sound—as if suddenly some girl was choked viciously.

Even choking, there was no mistaking the sugary sweet

voice of that awfully gorgeous and yet deathly-white-furred foxmite, Snow Frostbolt—or her twin sister Pearl.

With the ability to shift into an even more gorgeous human form—one of the most beautiful blonde human girls most guys had ever seen—that Snow and that Pearl, they both together lured foolish men to do even more foolish things like the wicked monsters they were.

Despite the claim Snow, that Pearl were both "tamed" and harmless.

Not "wild" and vicious like the rest of their kind.

But Greenstead Village? That was a human town about a month's journey southward. Was that near her own beastmite village? Or the last place she pretended to call home?

The Frostbolt sisters had only come to Saphold City a few months ago. No word from where.

And Maverick de Mayhem? Who was that? The name didn't sound like a beastmite name. No. More like a human boy's name, but—

"As you wish, m'lord," Snow said.

A sharp zing up Jacob's nose and down his spine. Magic. Real awful magic.

Magic the very stones of this church should protect him from.

But not for long. Jacob hurried even faster.

And faster.

"I summon thee," Snow said, "Flame of the Azura Blaze! Fly up and feast on human flesh and bone once more!"

First. For an instant. That smell of winter and lightning together.

A familiar smell lingering all too commonly around the younger boys all too eager to fall for the charms of Snow, or of Pearl, and who wanted to see their magic up close and personal.

A glance down and Jacob regretted the glance instantly.

A ball of blue flame curled and flowed upward in between the spiraling stairway.

Passing harmlessly by the pack of howling wolfmites and mewing tigermites.

Then the fireball expanded larger and larger. Gushing up through the stairway.

Till it crashed against the walls. The stairs.

And abruptly went out. As it the walls calmed its rage and vanquished its arcane horror.

Snow yelped?

"You bitch!" the ratling said. "Again! More power this time. He dies or you do—and that twin sister of yours replaces you as my spellblade concubine."

A spellblade? In other words Snow could shift into a magical blade. Her magical power could be wielded by whoever could wield her properly as a blade—but then why didn't the ratling wield Snow as a blade now?

But a concubine? Unless she was a wicked whore to that ratling and nothing more.

So both Frostbolt sisters were servants of that monster.

"As you wish, m'lord," Snow said, "But—ack!"

Snow gagged once again.

"But nothing!" the ratling said. "Kill him before he warns the town. Now!"

The pressure of her magic, like a weight heavy over all his body, was already was trying to slow him down, but no.

Jacob dashed up the stairs. Quicker than any of those monsters thought possible.

Even faster than the roaring bright fireball coming after him.

His feet had already memorized the way. Fast or slow didn't matter.

Thank the Lightful One he was already pulling the familiar rope once again.

Dong! Once!

Dong! Twice!

And one more—

CHAPTER I
MAVERICK DE MAYHEM

Sure the dark and stormy noon made the timing for the Festival of Flame and Passion here in Saphold City bad.

But not *that* bad.

His heart boomed as loud as the thunder outside. Mostly out of pure foolish hope.

Mostly out of pure foolish hope that maybe, more than friends, now, maybe—even if Maverick de Mayhem still hadn't heard from his dear childhood friend, Azura Blazehart, in the last few several months.

But no.

Maverick also hoped beyond hope that those wicked rumors of those dragon-worshipping monsters, and of beautiful girls, they all vanished to parts unknown, that all those rumors throughout Athedia were wrong, wrong, wrong, but no.

Not his dad.

Dad worried otherwise, and dad was a monster, technically, and secretly, hiding as a big brawny heroic guy, popular with the ladies, so to say, except (maybe) Azura and some elf girls like Peaches Fernhart and Cherry Appleseed.

So coming here together, father and son, claiming it was for the festival only ...

Least Saphold City should be safe. More than safe enough. For now.

From what exactly ... dad refused to say.

But here in Saphold, solid granite walls circled the entire city of concentrically spaced blocks of log cabins—cabins often two to five stories high. The stone wall was at least dozen paces thick and a few dozen paces high. Towering high enough to shield the buildings from view against larger monsters lurking nearby, even during in the depths of the darkest nights.

And, despite the many passages and rooms within it, the round wall was fashioned from solid granite boulders. Boulders each as large as a brawny human man if not larger.

A wall far stronger than steel. Thanks to dwarves like Uncle Spade.

So, of course, those stone walls should keep out the worst trouble outside of Saphold.

So no worries about the rain pelting the tiled roofs loud and clear—even the tiles along the steeply slanted rooftop many several paces above Maverick. The kind of rooftop that, during nice warm summer evenings back in Greenstead Village, Maverick loved to lounge on with friends.

Friends like Peaches Fernhart and Cherry Appleseed ... girls he really hoped were still safe.

Especially after hearing rumor after rumor of beautiful girls disappearing here and there and never being seen again.

Both Peaches and Cherry would love this festival. Maybe they'd sneak off and come here. Join Maverick secretly somehow as both claimed they'd would soon enough.

And that ... well ...

His short sky-blue hair with its dark-blue streaks, a hair color inherited from his elven mother, proved he had some elven blood in him so he had less to prove than the usual guy to an elf girl, to any elf girl.

Paces above the crisscrossing beams of pine logs around the notched ceiling. Beams with several glowing amber balls each about a foot wide, balls known as a bulbs, were embedded on the bottom of each plank.

Bulbs were a dwarven invention for lighting. Decent lightning—not too bright and not too dim—no matter the time of day or night. Its nature still secret to this very day.

But no matter.

Since if Peaches and Cherry did make it here ... his day would be brighter than any bulb.

Several rows and rows of long oak tables and benches filled the square room. Long and sturdy enough to seat several beefy people with some extra cozy space to spare. The wall of pale grey kegs loomed behind all the tables and held plenty of beer. The aisles by the walls and down the center. Wide enough for a pair of beefy men standing in place, dancing, shoulder-to-shoulder.

And thanks to the Festival of Flame and Passion plenty of young and not-so-young people here danced to fiddles, singers, and more. The mayhem was most mesmerizing. Plenty of gorgeous girls scantily clad in ultra-short skirts and cropped-short tops to dance with here.

Even, shockingly enough, a monster girl or few.

But then again, the notoriously all-girls magic academy, Witchengal Academy, accepted any girl with enough magical abilities to attend and attend safely—the city of Saphold upholding the right of those monster girls to stay here safe and sound too.

As long as they didn't go monster menace on anyone, at least.

Sure, since on top of being a woods guide, Maverick hunted monsters like beastmites and worse, for coin and more, parts for alchemist friends like his buddy Nate Wilhammer, and well ... Dad insisted Maverick learn to defend himself from monsters, especially beastmites, and actually encouraged Maverick go monster hunter.

Halfbreed, and even quarterbreeds going monster hunter —not exactly unusual either.

Even if they had elven blood in them—especially if they did. Better the hunter than the prey, dad liked to say.

But here, and now, woh.

Flirting and well, more, with a monster girl or few here ... very much possible, strangely enough.

And excitingly enough.

Like that erotically gorgeous foxmite of the snow-white furred kind. She spun around and around here and there across the room. Her long lush pale-golden hair swirled around with her. Hair down to her fine furry ass.

Wow. Just her figure. Gorgeously stunningly human—even her tits and ass.

Especially her tits and ass.

That fluffy fox tail from the nap of her back didn't detract from her beauty either. Not even how, instead of a human mouth and nose, she had a cute fox snout with a pink nose, and her head, a human-like head, not a canine-like head, no.

Sure her hands and feet were paw...ish, with sinister looking inch-long but very trim claws but ...

Those her huge fox ears from the top sides of her head, triangular ears a few inches big—really adorably cute.

And on top of the closest table that pair of tigermite girls dancing together.

Both as erotically gorgeous as the festive foxmite.

Both with suggestively ... placed(?) dark stripes all over their amazingly lush hourglass-to-heaven-and-back bodies. Bodies covered with short sleek fur.

So their stunningly amazing tits, ass, and figures—stuffed snuggly in bright lime-green ... underwear-in-public kind of outfits. Yeah. Each with an off-shoulder bra top of lime-green lace shoving up her amazing colossal chest, and matching skirt so short and snug it barely even covered her upper thighs—and what thighs they both had.

So many admirers in the crowd, a crowd surrounding the table, and obviously so, and why.

Despite their cute cat-like maws instead of human mouth and noses. Each with a tiger-like tail from the nap of her back. Their pair of huge triangular cat ears from the top sides of their human-like head, poking out of their hair.

And the amber-furred beauty to the left had chest-long wedges of gorgeous golden hair.

The orange-furred beauty to the right. She had bright-scarlet-red curled over her right shoulder and down hanging over her right breast.

Yet unlike the festive foxmite their pawish hands and feet had no visible claws ... out.

So wow. Yeah.

Especially whenever they, together, gracefully leapt with the music to another nearby table. Seeking out more guys to seduce.

To tumble onto their drunk lusting asses.

Next there'd be clawgirls dancing around in their lizard girl form—as in scaled skin and segmented claws for hands and feet. Or lamias—half human, half snake girls and ... sigh.

Keep dreaming, Azura would so say.

And Dad, he'd just burst out laughing, since why not? A festival was a festival.

Never mind Maverick inherited both his dad's forms, this human one and the not-so-human but, well, Maverick, like his dad, could shift into a wolfmite.

A black-furred green-eyed wolfmite.

So yeah. Awkward.

Especially if any of those beastmite girls scented the real truth about him, or his dad.

CHAPTER 2
MAVERICK DE MAYHEM

Okay, okay, judging by how many guys—both human and elven—tried to dance with that erotically gorgeous pair of tigermite girls. Some even succeeding for longer than expected before falling off the table ... wow.

The expressions of those tigermite girls ... clearly enjoying all the attention.

How often that festive foxmite beauty danced with a new lustsmitten stud every few moments before twirling away to the next stud, and then the next stud ... dodging girls and guys as easily as she seduced every guy in the room ...

Definitely trouble ... Azura would so want to smack sense into Maverick and sigh.

Focus. Priorities were priorities ... finding Azura came first.

After all, when Azura left Greenstead Village behind for

"reasons" and, supposedly, came here to Saphold City for training in that magical academy, Witchengal Academy—a famous, more like a notoriously girls' only academy for witches, sorceresses, and such.

Least she claimed that was why she left Greenstead so suddenly.

But no one here in Witchengal had heard of Azura.

Good thing his best buddy, five foot two inches of the finest dwarf guy, Drake Anvil, was here too. Right now Drake sought any hint or rumor of Azura from within the dwarven section of Saphold.

Just wait here at Tail's Tavern for Drake to return. Party if you want, even with the beautiful beastmites girls here since why not. They might even enjoy a little rowdy hunter and hunted role play of the chained up and sexy fun kind.

Uh huh ... but no.

Even if Dad and Drake approved how could Maverick party when Drake was out searching and Azura herself was still missing?

So no.

Even if Dad had insisted Maverick dress like all the other guys. Shirtless and wearing only loose-sleeved slacks.

No shirts. None.

Unarmed too—except for what was inside his blue-leather pouch. Big enough to hold two fists inside it but, instead, he carried three chain whips of extra-light but extra-strong titan steel.

Each whip could shackle a monster securely. Wrap the creature in chains and then use the sturdy latch near the handle's end to hook, to then lock and tighten the chain securely in place.

Or use the short thin blade on its end to finish the monster off.

Or, thanks to his alchemist buddy Nate, if the monster was magical enough, Maverick could utter the right incantation and then transmute the captive monster into a magical weapon known as a spellblade. Wield whatever power they had as his own through the blade.

Especially beastmite girls of the magical sort, so of course, Maverick also had three muzzles of sturdy leather as well in there.

All hidden within his pouch of course—but easily snatched out and still very usable.

Never mind Maverick also mastered (mostly) the beastmite martial art known as Razorine, thanks to Dad and all that secret training, in both human and wolfmite form, so …

Huh?

In the far dark corner to the right. Three brawny-looking men huddled together. Hidden within their own shadowy dark-blue cloaks and hoods? Not half-naked like most of the people here.

Least they looked like men. The shadows hid whatever they were well enough.

And judging by those beastmite girls dancing out in the wide obvious open, clearly it wasn't just humans, elves, and dwarves who came to this tavern.

Well, openly at least.

Since that tingle down his back ... that tense urge to fight, prove himself ... no.

Those shadowy men meant trouble. Trouble Maverick better be ready for and—woh!

A coy giggle and that festive foxmite girl swirled right in front of Maverick.

And stayed in front of him?!

Okay, okay, maybe she needed a quick ... wow, just as a breeze of her fox scent, oh my wow, it hit his face like a spear of flaming wow.

Her lush pale-golden hair swirled around her as much as her long fluffy fox tail. No missing her lush legs. Legs he'd love to ... you know with. Slender arms raised high. Pawish hands together.

Her face ... very human...ish, enough.

She winked at him with her giant azure-blue eyes—both streaked with sparkling sky blue, and, of course, instead of a human mouth and nose she had that slim fox snout a few inches long ending with a lovely pink nose.

Which she licked very suggestively at that very moment.

Just like, instead of human ears she had a pair of giant fox ears—each a few inches big, as in nearly as big as his own human hands—and on the top sides of her head. Poking out of her long hair. Their insides a lovely pink.

Ears that twitched up excited once then twice.

No mistaking how she wiggled and swayed her curvy slim figure. A figure so erotically gorgeous. To heaven and back, as Dad would say.

Despite her short and beautifully sleek snow-white fur.

No missing how amazingly sexy her hourglass-to-heaven-and-back figure was. Hard not to leer at her more than he should. Leer and lower his guard and—woh.

Apparently bare-in-the-freaking-sexy fur too.

Even that stunningly ginormous chest.

Especially that ginormous chest. Heavenly endowed, as Dad would say—just like everyone called Azura's chest. Her heaven-and-back figure as well.

Peaches and Cherry too, but elf girls ... well ... what elf girl wasn't shockingly beautiful?

So beautiful they were touchy about being touched by anyone "unworthy" but Maverick, with his half elven blood, was at least worthy enough to speak with them regularly since childhood but ... sigh.

But this festive foxmite, her giant jiggling kind of heavenly endowed chest. The kind that caused wagons to crash. Pile up kind of crash. Especially in the woods—where raiding the crashed wagons—very likely by other beastmites.

One of the many traditions his dad had outright rejected, and got exiled for that rejection.

No longer swirling but dancing and swaying and wiggling right in front of Maverick, the festive foxmite girl giggled playfully again.

Winking again at him again. Her giant azure-blue eyes, their sparkling sky-blue streaks, now gazing right into his. No hesitation. No worries. Just pure delightful fun.

"You next?" she said.

Her voice. Also like the sweetest candy made into sound —but strangely, kinda familiar too, kinda like Azura, like when she went all giggly cutesy but ... Azura was human, very much human, not a foxmite, and never this festive of a girl either.

Her foxy scent ...no, in his human form, well, human noses were more decoration than well ...

Still. Gulp was all too right.

"To fight?" Maverick said. "Or to fuck?"

"Both!" the festive foxmite said. "I've always wanted to taste a real hunter!"

And she licked his lips—as if she hadn't licked plenty of lips before—with that beastmite kiss of affection—or seduction, and revealing his elven blood to her, no doubt, and maybe, even, his wolfmite blood too.

"I'm Snow," she said, "Snow Frostbolt."

Just as her pawish cute hands slipped down gently onto the sides of his shoulders. Then down smoothly, sensually along his sides. To resting on the sides of his waist.

"Maverick," he said, "Maverick de Mayhem."

And he slipped his hand over her shoulders. Furry soft and slid down her silky soft sides combing her gorgeously soft fur down until he rested his palms over her swaying hips.

"Seduce and slash," Maverick said, "all too simple for a beauty like you, Snow."

The festive foxmite girl let out a cute cackle as sweet as the most sugary candy.

"I **so** know," Snow said, "That annoying Chieftain of mine *so* insists I go bait girl to lure humans and elves to their doom. You know. Make wagons crash using my girlie charm, he-he, and other stupidly awful stuff."

"You don't have to," Maverick said.

"Of course!" Snow said. "And get exiled like that Night Fang wolfmite years ago ... or submit to be spellbladed."

"But stay here ..." Maverick said.

She pouted dejectedly. Ears sinking too, some, as if she really meant it.

"And get spellbladed too," Snow said, "but least I get to choose who wields me, he-he."

And her sensual wink wink at him—a hint hint that he might be the lucky winner.

Uh huh. No wonder her tribe let her attend the academy. She'd serve them as a better spellblade in the end. Shifting between seduce and slash femme fatale and deadly magical blade bound to serve and obey her wicked wielder.

But not his problem.

(Yet.)

So Maverick gave her gorgeous hourglass-to-heaven-and-back figure another look down and up and woh.

Not bare in thee fur but close. Really really close.

Dressed in the skimpiest snow-white lace. That off-shoulder bra top of stretchy snug lace somehow also shoved her amazing breasts up at him. That supershort supersnug skirt showed as much of her lace panties as it covered.

Yeah.

Risqué to thee extreme and wow, Maverick couldn't help but like her for it.

"Wow," Maverick said, "that lace matches your fur perfectly."

Snow purred. "Exactly! Wanna see how easily it comes off?"

This time Maverick let out a playfully lusting laugh.

"Snow, you've got the seduce part down pat," Maverick said. "At this rate you'll end me quicker than you can lick me."

Snow barked another laugh.

"End you?" She said. "Ooo, Mavs, I already like you too much to end, he-he."

Then she smirked sexy wicked.

"So more talkie talkie talkie," Snow said, "or dancie dancie dancie?"

A moment later she had her answer.

CHAPTER 3
BLIZZARD CLAWSTORM

Sitting with his cloaked back to the solid log wall in back of this human tavern, and with the awful noise of the human menace celebrating all around him, Blizzard Clawstorm did his best not to snarl at that wretched Snow Frostbolt, that wretched tribe concubine-to-be, that spellblade-to-be.

His spellblade-to-be, soon enough.

Dancing, flirting, **licking** every single human and elf guy here without a care in this wicked world.

Especially her wretched target—Maverick de Mayhem.

No mistaking that boy's freakishly sky-blue hair and its dark-blue streaks—even across the room. That elf-blooded mutt of a boy. The best kind of prey for a beastmite huntress to prove herself worthy of real respect.

The muggy heat of this place, this rugged hot tavern was nothing compared to the rage that was building inside him.

The stink of alcohol only weakened the guard of these lesser creatures, these humans and elves, these prey thinking they were more than mere prey.

Far in front of him, on the other side tavern, two tigermite bitches dared danced on top of a long table for the amusement of their wickedly weak prey. Their charms were for luring prey to their doom, not entertaining their prey.

That they dressed as near bare-in-the-fur as their prey dressed near naked ...

All wretches. All needed a proper lesson in the hunt.

But the signal hadn't gone off yet. The signal for the attack to commence.

The two dongs that would have warned the town had been delayed by Pearl and her magic—thanks to their ratling war chief acting in time—and turned that signal into a herald this city's coming doom.

But her attempts at treachery, they proved her unworthy.

As unworthy as the filthy piss water and fish stew this place served to its lesser patrons.

Now Pearl was the left of two spellblades strapped to his waist. A azure-blue bladed saber a few feet long snuggly wrapped in dark-blue elf-skin leather. Letting him wield, create and control, not just ice but ice-natured lightning and flame.

Lightning and flame that burned cold not hot.

His first spellblade was already strapped to his waist, and ready to be drawn.

A scarlet-bladed saber a few feet long wrapped in crimson human-skin leather. Forged from the scarlet foxmite witch Rosaline who had also attended Witchengal. An overly beautiful witch who had been too cocky for her own gorgeous good, all thanks to her incredible skill in creating and controlling her scarlet flames.

Daring to defy her betters. Only seduce, not slash a certain pathetic dwarf boy. A boy nowhere to be found now. Fled like the coward he was.

So Rosaline was reduced to a blade, a spellblade who could only obey as she should.

And nothing more. Just like Pearl now.

Not even worthy as bed warmers. Those unworthy bitches hadn't killed a single human or elven guy on their own. Nothing to prove their worthiness as huntresses, and now, never will.

The signal to crush this city. Soon it should come.

Soon.

Even with this bench creaking all too loudly under him, the fiddles were more than loud enough to hid the noise.

Distract the prey from their coming doom.

No chance the spells woven into this clothing would be seen through. Not by such drunks and careless pathetic things.

Blizzard hadn't even bothered to shift into a human form. He still struggled with at stupid feat.

But no matter.

This cloak and hood, its magic, hid him well enough. Hid his two companions too.

For now they sat beside him. On each side.

The magic those twin foxmite witches Pearl and Snow wove into these cloaks worked wonders.

Not even the slightest suspicion. Yet. Not from any of the prey around them.

Drunk or sober.

It alone proved their time at that academy wasn't entirely wasted—but their tribe-trained witches still knew far more than they did. That they both already dared disobey their ratling war chief, Lord Bonecrusher, once already ...

Blizzard better prepare for the worst. Snow may betray them as well.

Be ready to reduce her to a spellblade no better than the two he currently wore, and wielded.

After all her childhood mission to watch over that wretched halfbreed and that exiled wolfmite in that human village, that Night Fang, didn't go as planned ... a failure, mostly. Thanks to her and her kindred getting far too friendly with her targets.

But Blizzard had the dragon egg ready. In his hands. Under his cloak.

An egg a foot wide and a bright divinely sky blue. Within it a dragon ready and rearing to raze this section of town to the ground. Using its divine blue flame. Flame that should be able to burn through any blade or magic.

Except spellblades blessed by its divine bloodline—like the two he wielded.

Soon it would burn down and feast on all the prey it could catch.

CHAPTER 4
MAVERICK DE MAYHEM

Maverick and Snow. They swirled in each other's arms. Around and around and around.

No hesitation now.

The muggy heat. Nothing compared to the passionate heat between them.

The alcohol thick in the air. From loads of bittersweet ale and fresh foamy beer.

Nowhere as intoxicating as Snow and her foxy sweet scent.

The thunder rumbling over the fiddles, songsters, and overall cheer—nothing compared to the pounding of his lust-smitten heart.

Even the plank floor. As smooth as each of Snow's graceful yet swift steps. Swaying herself, and Maverick around couple after couple. Slipping passed guys and girls of the human and elven sorts, all glancing their way, all also dancing to the fast fiddle tunes.

Until the fiddles stopped once again—for a few moments.

Surrounded by people still dancing anyway ...

Just as Snow slipped her fluffy fox tail around his rear. Nice and cozy and yet firm, since beastmite tails—including one of a foxmite like Snow—were often used as deadly clubs in battle.

Even his own—whenever Maverick took on his wolfmite form.

"Your tail," Maverick said, "is much better as a lovely ass warmer than as a club."

"Exactly!" Snow said. "I'm an even better body warmer alive and cuddling."

Snow wiggled her shoulders, and her chest one again, rubbing those heavenly endowed breasts against his own chest more than merely slightly.

Bad enough his foolish eyes sank back down toward her stunningly ginormous breasts, at the stretchy snug lace shoving those giant heavenly endowed wowzies upward at him. How those off-shoulder straps stretched nicely and yet didn't interfere at all with her graceful movements ...

A throaty giggle and smirky smile Snow pulled him closer to her. Pressing her ginormous chest against his. Rubbing him there to heavenly bliss.

Close enough to feel how warm she really was. Smell how clean her breath really was ...

"Nice minty breath there, Snow," Maverick said.

Her purr loud and sensually clear ... obviously she scented how much he wanted her right here and now too.

And his elven blood too. Very tasty to a beastmite.

But his wolfmite blood ... she really didn't mind a half-breed? Somehow he found that hard to believe. Beastmites he encountered during his monster hunts ...

Only scorn for his halfbreed nature.

And sleeping together, Maverick and Snow, together here and now ... without any seduce and slash successes yet she might suffer more than mere exile but ... hard to resist her. The real rare chance of bedding a genuine foxmite girl of the sexiest kind.

More intoxicating than the alcohol thick in the air.

"A real cutie," Snow said, "and complimenting little cute me ... Mavs, you so definitely wanna chain me up and have your way with me, don't you?"

Uh huh. So his buddy Drake nailed it again.

A festive was a festive, after all, so fiddles and good cheer. Thump thump thump went so many people around them. To the music and not. It wasn't just the air that felt hot now.

So Maverick matched her smutty smirk with one of his own. Swaying his hips with hers once again.

"Muzzle you too," Maverick said, "but that voice of yours, that snout, too cute to muzzle."

And he pecked her pink nose quick but decisively.

But then, that instant, Snow shoved him backwards? Quick and just as decisively.

Unlike a real fight—where he would have pulled her along with him, maybe used her to cushion his fall, no, like his dad would say, a festival was a festival, so Maverick went with her shove, stumbling backwards as gracefully as he could.

Stumbling until his knees smacked ... a bench?

His ass flopped down. On that bench? A. The. Bench behind him. Paces ahead of him--and close behind Snow. Another bench and table. With people dancing on it. He was behind the table before the wall he had just been standing by a little while ago.

And yet. No.

Maverick had been so too unaware of his surroundings. Not good. Snow was getting to him. In a dangerous way.

Very dangerous way.

The purrs and giggles and no doubt about it. Those beautiful tigermite girls danced right behind him now. No mistaking their feline scent either. Their giggles and another thump of another admirer falling to keep up with them. Falling on his ass or tumbling down to the bench. The bench on the other side of this long table.

Especially when, an instant later, Snow twirled over to him, landed her fine furry ass nice and purrfectly onto his now-extra warm and blissful lap. Hooked her left arm around his head.

And gave his face a nice mouthful of her furry warm breast—and only that lovely fine stretchy thin lace between him and more of that that furry festive heaven.

The fiddlers fiddled up more rapid tunes. Cheers broke out.

Thump thump thumps of people thumping the floor for more more more.

While with another sensual purr Snow rubbed the bottom of her head against the top of his. Her long lush hair blanketing him over his right side. As if the celebration was far away—not blazing right around them both.

"Ooo," Snow said, "you **are** so happy to feel me, he-he."

She then wiggled her rear against his hips. No doubt feeling, and enjoying, just how big and hard his manhood had ... you know.

So Maverick hugged Snow around her soft supple and sexy bare waist. Pulling her closer.

"More than merely happy," Maverick said.

"Enough to," Snow said, "save me from some trouble? Seduce is all fun and games but slash ... you don't have to but ..."

"Wow," Maverick said. "Kinda sneaky there, Snow."

Okay, okay. He needed to be as hard as the bench creaking against his ass, not as soft as Snow's furry ass on his lusting happy lap, but ... wowzie, was Snow had to resist right now.

So Maverick gave Snow a genuine cuddly hug.

"Still," he said. "Very tempting."

"But?" Snow said.

He then gave her rear a nice hard slap, and wow, did her ass feel fine. Almost fine enough to go along with whatever trouble she intended to drag him into—likely as her target to slay all to win respect within her tribe and whatnot.

She jolted in place, with a shocked gasp, but didn't try to flee, or even struggle against him.

Yet.

"Bad girl," he said, "trying to lure my foolish cute rear to its doom so soon ..."

"Heeeeey," Snow said.

"Hay is for horses," Maverick said, "and I would have been your stallion but—"

Snow pouted—no missing that silly sight despite his face-full of furry boob. Her ears sank enough to even tickle the top of his head.

And she gulped. Clearly nervous.

So Maverick gave her another cuddly hug around her waist. Dad did say saving the damsel-in-distress wasn't the worse way to go ... in more ways than one.

"But I *do* mean it," Snow said. "Chain me up and ravish me all you want if I don't."

"Oh really now?" Maverick said. "I'll chain you all up now and spellblade you—"

"Spellblade me now," Snow said, "and ravish me later all you want!"

That ... Maverick gulped. Hesitating. Since ... so tempting since she actually volunteered for the spellblading and sexy time. But ... trust. He'd have to trust her unless he bound her with the chain—or at the very least was the only one to say the incantation while she ... she ...

No.

Azura would so smack him senseless if he did fall for this trick—once they found her, that was, but Drake ... ack!

His pouch wiggled—from Snow reaching in and slipping out ... woh.

A chain?! The rattle in front of him said it all.

Snow face-fulled Maverick even more with her furry boob bliss—now covering his eyes.

Very much covering his whole entire face now.

And she kept him from seeing how Snow actually handled the chain itself but no mistaking those metallic rattles ... she already had it coiled on her lap and was examining the handle in her pawishly cute hands.

"Ooo," Snow said, "*niiiice* chains. Nate really outdid himself. So what's the incantation this time?"

"Nate?" Maverick said, "how'd you know ... wait."\

Snow giggled. "Just realizing *now* who I am? I should smack you for being so dense."

"But ... Azura," Maverick said. "Azura—"

"Call me Snow," she said. "I'll explain later."

"But ..." Maverick said, "how ... how did you hide your foxmite side from me so well, and so long and dad ... no, does dad know? He had to smell the true about you but why ... why did—ack!"

Her tail smacked his bottom? Like a playful but dangerous spanking with a club. Jolting the shock out of him.

Some.

"Later!" Snow said. "Now tell me the incantation, and quickly!"

"But I ..." Maverick said.

He gulped. He'd have to trust her but why ... no. If Snow. No. Azura was Snow. Snow was Azura. Their voice. All too similar. He should have ... have no. Don't focus on the past. Focus on the present.

Focus on now.

So call her Snow. Yeah. Snow. Azura ... no. Focus now. On what's important.

Behind him. A few tables down. To his right. There. Those weird shadowy men in the corner of the room. That danger by the line of kegs. The real danger.

Probably.

His hackles. Beyond tingling now.

"Nate he ..." Maverick said, "you won't be bound, won't be slaved if you're not bound by the chain, and ..."

"I know!" Snow said. "And I can transform back by my own will if I say the incantation with you."

"So Nate knew?" Maverick said. "Who else—ack!"

Snow. Azura. Whoever she really was, this festive foxmite spanked his rear again with her tail. No holding back either.

Very much an Azura-level smacking. Even making the bench squeak more than a bit.

Wobble them both too.

"Later I said!" Snow said. "Incantate now!"

Yeah. Snow. Azura. Sigh.

She wanted him to call her Snow, least for now. And she wouldn't submit to the slaved kind of spellblading no ... never to spellblading period, not unless she really was desperate and ... he'd soon need a spellblade.

Really soon.

A beastmite witch free versus that very same beastmite witch as a spellblade—the spellblade would definitely win each and every time in terms of outright powerful and such.

But slaved spellblades couldn't help any other way

though. The wielder would control, have to control the creation and manipulation of whatever magic the spellblade casted.

Free spellblades can wield their abilities on their own—but need some help from their wielder for the full boosting effect.

So probably against those shadowy men—and maybe more.

Serious trouble then,

"Okay, okay," Maverick said. "Here it is."

Maverick took a deep breath full of festive foxy scent and, well, her furry boob still in his face. Thumping his heart far too crazy. His slacks ...

No.

Not now.

"Bind this vexing vixen," Maverick said, "into the best spellblade a guy can grab and grope!"

Snow actually said it with him—and giggled right at the end.

"Figures," Snow said. "A pervy incantation for you pervy guys. So you better start groping me, and more after—"

An instant later Snow vanished.

Gone.

Replaced by a gorgeous azure-blue-bladed saber across his lap. A few feet long. Curved up slightly to the tip. Balanced perfectly and lighter than ... wow, Maverick. His mouth.

Dry.

"Snow?" he said. "Azura?"

"Yay!" she said. "It worked! And call me Snow! Snow Frostbolt! You'll soon see why!"

Her voice came from the blade itself. That she … she really went spellblade for him—a free, not slaved, spellblade but an actual spellblade. For him. To wield.

He gulped.

Mouth still dry. No furry boob to excuse his thumping lusting heart now.

No matter how loud those fiddles were getting. Louder and louder. Thumps from dancers even louder and louder. How he could even hear anything but music and thumps was amazing in itself.

"Okay, okay," Maverick said. "I—"

"Leave the magic to me," Snow said, "and I'll leave the physical combat to you, and to those tigermite cuties Amber and Scarlet, right girls? You know what to do!"

"Okay, but—" Maverick said. "Wait. Those tigermite girls—"

"Of course we do!" both tigermite girls said.

Both of them. Together. Right behind and beside him? As in sitting on their knees on the table to his sides. Since when, when did they both get so close? So cuddling close.

Killing strike distance too—if things went badly, but … no. Azura wouldn't. Her friends.

No.

But his monster hunter skill … seduced pathetically nonexistent was all too right.

Just as, suddenly, his head, it was sandwiched between two stunning pairs of amazingly massively tigermite breasts.

Only their green lace bra tops saved him from complete and utter sexual-induced shock.

Amber giggled. "You really didn't recognize us?"

"Such a *baaad* boy," Scarlet said. "We did say we'd met up with you, remember?"

Their voices ... and ... no. But it had to be. And. That promise. Over a month ago but.

"Amber," he said. "You're Peaches, and Scarlet—you're Cherry?!"

"Yup!" both tigermite girls said together.

"So Amber to my left," he said, "Scarlet to the right. And. And. And."

"And if you want to harem us," Amber said. "If you want all the touchie touchie touchie you can ever handle, and more, lots more ... and as tigermites no need to hold back, he-he."

"And I **know** you do, wolf boy," Scarlet said. "It's a beast-mite guy thing, of course, and you'll get touchie touchie rights in both our forms, right Amber?"

Amber giggled so happily. "Right! So better be a good hunter hero boy."

Scarlet sighed oh-so-sensually. "And save our sexy cute rears from—"

DONG!

The bell. From a nearby chapel?

But it shouldn't ring today. Never on festival days—whether in this city or any other place.

Not unless ... trouble, serious trouble, as in the monster kind usual, but—

CHAPTER 5
MAVERICK DE MAYHEM

Dong! Again. The bell. From a nearby chapel.

Maverick. His heart.

It must have skipped a beat.

No.

More than a beat.

Several.

No missing that signal. Signal of serious trouble. Monster trouble, probably.

Monsters like Azura—no, Like Snow, Amber, and Scarlet but ... would they really join some kind of attack here in Saphold?

No. Maverick. He.

But Amber and Scarlet tensed up—no missing it. Not from how much the bench squeaked underneath him suddenly. How much the tables shifted against his back. From their weight suddenly shifting closer to him.

Even with their amazing boobs sandwiching his face—no missing their scent of fear.

No missing the sudden silence of the fiddles.

Of the crowd itself.

Utter utter silence. The whole entire tavern.

Cautious quiet.

No festive anything at the moment. None.

But not even rain pounded the tiled ceiling anymore. Nothing. No wind howled outside. No thumping from feet anywhere let alone from window shutters banging outside.

Nothing.

And with Snow, how Snow volunteered to go sexy spell-blade for him right there and then, only moments ago, and then Amber and Scarlet offering to go harem honeys for him if he saved them from ... from, oh no.

Maverick jumped to his feet. Spellblade in his right hand.

Amber and Scarlet held onto his sides gently, but cuddly tenderly, but also nervously. Their breasts now pillowing his arms so heart thumpingly wonderfully ...

Their claws could easily shred him dead this very instant but no, they hung onto him for protection. As if their abilities, whatever they were, they wouldn't be enough to save themselves.

So okay, yeah—he'd accept all three beautiful beastmite girls as his harem honeys.

Snow.

Amber.

Scarlet.

Save them whatever slash tradition they wanted to avoid —and stick only with seduce.

Especially seducing him.

But the light. The light itself somehow dimmed?

From the dwarf bulbs along the crisscrossing beams above them all. They shouldn't suddenly dimmed. No. Dwarf-made bulbs never dimmed. Ever. They never failed in any way unless damaged severely or … some kind of magic was dimming the light in here.

An attack.

An attack had already begun—inside this very tavern.

No wonder Snow needed to be spellbladed so quickly.

No wonder Amber and Scarlet clung onto him—someone with actual combat experience.

And a strong willingness to help them—trust them and—

No time left.

Maverick turned around. Toward those shadowy men in back. In the corner. Near the kegs.

Just as the howls of three deranged wolfmites erupted from that very corner.

From those shadowy men.

The biggest and brawniest howled the loudest. From the center. Between the other two brawny men.

No.

Now three brawny wolfmites cloaked and hooded. Mottle gray fur underneath now the two smaller hoods and cloaks.

Pure deathly white underneath the biggest one. The center one.

And the fur—before he hadn't spotted any fur or wolf bits

on the shadowy men before—despite the good light. So ... those outfits, maybe spelled to make them look more like men, and keep them from drawing attention as well as some kind of condition was met.

Which meant those wolfmites struggled to shift into human, or elven forms.

"Snow!" the deathly-white wolfmite said. "You treacherous bitch! I'll spellblade you into slavery with your own twin sister! Amber. Scarlet. Hold that target down or else you'll join the other traitors as—"

Both Amber and Scarlet mewed loud and clearly—at the biggest wolfmite in the corner.

"Never!" Amber said. "If we do help kill anyone it'll be you, Blizzard!"

Scarlet even hissed fiercely at the biggest wolfmite.

"Mav is our mate now!" Scarlet said. "We rather die than be your killer honeys!"

Smiling grimly Maverick gave them a curt nod. No questions about trust now. The fury on that wolfmite's face. On the face of all three of those wolfmites.

Amber and Scarlet clearly threw their lot in with Maverick—no turning back.

Just as the biggest wolfmite, the deathly-white wolfmite, drew a pair of colorful blades. One exactly like the spellblade Snow shifted into, the spellblade in Maverick's right hand.

Like a twin blade.

In the wolfmite's left hand was another similar blade—but the blade was scarlet-red, not blue?

"The blue spellblade," Snow said, "is my twin sis Pearl.

The scarlet spellblade is my litter sis Rosaline. If we can save them ..."

"We'll save them," Maverick said. "I'll take on Blizzard. Amber, Scarlet, hold off his buddies until—"

Amber giggled, but not happily this time.

"We'll do more," Amber said, "than hold those bums off, right Scarlet?"

"Right!" Scarlet said. "We're not helpless little cute kittens."

Snow cried out. From the spellblade's blade again.

"Exactly!" Snow said. "Now let's go and—"

BOOM!!!

From the right. Paces beyond the tavern's very own log wall.

From the building next to them.

Followed by screams of terror and death.

CHAPTER 6
DRAKE ANVIL

Drake Anvil bashed down and smashed in enough beastmite brains to know the intense downpour here should have deterred their attack everywhere throughout Saphold City.

Not intensified it.

But no amount of thunder booming nearby could drown out all their bestial battle cries.

Wolfmites howled louder than the cursing gales of wind—not even his beard—as thick with water as it was—could resist those violent gales.

The thick-with-brawn tigermites before Drake roared louder than the rivers of rainwater roaring through the streets to their left.

Streets so flooded that now they gushed like violent canals.

Not streets.

All thanks to the pace-high curbs, and raised sidewalks of solid smooth granite, meant to protect pedestrians from speeding wagons. Curbs common in many dwarf-made settlements of any real size for the last few hundred years.

Lightning flashed as quickly as the steel claws his war hammer deflected from his face and gut. Razor sharp and thin claws covered in blood and worse—likely from innocent bystanders.

Not warriors like himself.

Worst of all—the shrieks of a giant rat thirsting for blood and battle.

But not a rat.

No.

Worse. Far worse. A ratling.

A ratling full of battle lust. For the blood of those weaker than them.

Its cries were far shriller than any rain crashing down on the many tiled rooftops and their pace-wide awnings. Those cries echoed down all the many alleyways. Alleyways drier than the sidewalks by the streets—leaving no worthwhile trail. The awnings themselves protected the alleys from the worst of the rain.

But only a ratling could drive this horde of beastmites to attack during this savage storm.

And that hollow tint to that shrill cry. That whiney growl.

No doubt.

The very same ratling that stole the love of his life. Enslaved that wonderful, that lovely foxmite Rosaline into a savage spellblade. All because she dared refused to slash him,

Drake Anvil, her beloved dwarf boy dead—her life for his instead.

So Drake swore on his beard he'd find her. Save her.

Somehow.

And today would be that day.

Doing it while also helping out Maverick and Azura—a nice double treat.

Especially since Azura—that she turned out to be a foxmite in hiding that ... well, ended up being an adorable sweetheart a lot like his own beloved Rosaline ...

Good for Maverick—if he didn't mess up the reunion too badly.

Good for Peaches and Cherry too—if they didn't overdo their elven side too much, or let their tigermite beauty get to their pretty little heads, and overdo the surprise in the wrong kind of way.

So Drake bashed more tigermite bastards into the gushing canals that were once streets.

Their screams, Their cries.

Drake had as little mercy for them as those raging currents.

The cries of the ratling. The ratling was close.

Within a block or two close—

BOOM!!!

An explosion a cabin down the street?! So close!

The cries of humans and elves suddenly loud and clear.

No. Not an explosion.

Not of thunder or lightning.

No. But a door being destroyed—and that ratling, that

ratling who dubbed himself Lord Bonecrusher, he was to blame.

And must be stopped—now.

With a battle cry of his own Drake slammed through more walls of incoming tigermites. Risking life and limb to reach that ratling as soon as dwarvenly possible, to reach its latest scene of horror, and crush that ratling, revenge his sweetheart, and save her, his dear beloved Rosaline.

Save her today like she saved him only months ago.

CHAPTER 7
MAVERICK DE MAYHEM

That loud boom from the building next to the tavern. The screams following it.

It changed everything.

Maverick needed to finish this mess of trouble here, in this tavern, and quickly.

No mistaking the sudden musty smell of shattered pine—even as it came from next door. The sudden crash of rain smashing down hard, and harder, very suddenly.

Not more quiet. Not now.

Just more screams of terror.

Screams inducing whimpers of fear among those within this tavern.

The sudden gales of savage wind blasted the log walls of this tavern. Making them squeal and creak. Blasted stronger than any regular thunderstorm Maverick ever encountered. Too convenient—for the enemy.

No missing that the even more savage stink of rat—more like ratling.

Humans. Elves. Beside Maverick they all trembled. Least the people Maverick could still see in the dim light. His half-beastmite nature helped him here. He could see better than most human in dim light.

But the humans, the elves they still squeezed toward the walls. Fearfully.

The girls, scantily clad or not, were surrounded protectively by the men, whether human or elf, whether brawny, wiry or fat, or even pathetically slim. None of the men acted cowardly.

Despite Maverick being the only armed one among them.

Good. Saphold was a good place.

A good place to save.

But now the fight was more than between those three enraged, and well armed, wolfmites. And next door, a ratling so well armed those dings of rain against steel armor, loud enough to hear through the log walls. Into here.

And Maverick's own companions. Unarmed—and very much scantily clad.

Only so much they could do against an armored foe like that ratling. With only regular claws and fang to defend them against actual steel claws and magical steel blades.

Not a good matchup—for Maverick and his newfound honeys Amber and Scarlet.

Even with Snow as his spellblade.

Next door the ratling screamed out strange sounding but vile curses.

And the dwarf bulbs crisscrossing the planks above them. They all turned dark that very moment. As if broken beyond repair.

All within this tavern. Probably the building next door too.

Maybe all over Saphold.

More fell magic—unlike the lovelier magic Snow no doubt wielded, and the witches that attended Witchengal.

That ratling had command of some magic. So even more dangerous.

And even more important that Maverick finish this Blizzard wolfmite and his companions here and now.

Least Maverick could now wield Snow's magic, with her help, even if he wasn't sure what kind of magic she used, what nature favored her, and whatnot.

And unlike those wolfmites, Amber and Scarlet as tigermites could shadowjump, could blend into the shadows and jump between shadows, teleport between shadows, and even better now—with so many dark shadows thanks to the broken bulbs and the darkness of the storm.

Amber mewed. Mewed frightfully fiercely at the wolfmites.

"Mavs," Amber said, "leave those wolvies to us! The shadows give us the advantage now!"

"Exactly!" Scarlet said. "Go help the people next door!"

Even in the dim light Maverick could make out how Scarlet held her pawish hands up near his face, and very much claws out and wiggling excited now.

Very trim and very razor sharp claws. All soon to help him.

"We know a trick or two ourselves," Scarlet said. "Besides magic from Witchengal. So go crush Lord Bonecrusher and the rest will panic, and run away!"

Maverick gave them both a curt nod and smiled. Especially at how their big cute eyes smiled back with their sweet feline maws.

"I'll crush him for both of you," Maverick said, "and Snow here as—"

Mews came from above them. Above Maverick. Above Amber and Scarlet too.

Tigermite mews of the feminine feline kind.

Over a dozen of them.

CHAPTER 8
MAVERICK DE MAYHEM

But Maverick refused to curse his fate, his situation—he was alive. Still.

All his girlfriends too.

Snow. Amber. Scarlet.

That Snow was Azura ... after all this time he found Azura in the least expected way possible and yet ... his hope was true, that she felt more than mere friendship toward him ... even more, especially now.

So no time to lose to these monster scum now.

But all along the crisscrossing beams of the tavern's ceiling. The darkness hid the pack of tigermite girls. Over a dozen of them. Scattered across the beams above them. The ceiling beams crisscrossing the space above them.

Paces above them.

And no mistaking those mews erupting louder and

louder, As if Maverick and his companions weren't worthy of an mere ambush.

No.

They needed to impose fear and hopelessness into their potential prey.

A foolish decision—something Maverick himself learned long ago.

Just like the fear that pack of tigermites imposed on the party-goers squeezed against the walls of the tavern. All silent. All definitely certain Maverick was their only hope.

Maverick and their only two tigermite allies, Amber and Scarlet.

Blizzard and his two wolfmites lingered in that corner. Between the wall of kegs and the log wall.

As if wary of Maverick and his newfound spellblade. Of Snow.

A wise decision—but not wise enough!

"Traitors deserve death!"

From one of the tigermite girls right above Maverick.

"Die!" another tigermite girl said. "Die like that boy should have—by claw and fang!"

Amber huffed. "You brats are just jealous."

Scarlet chuckled. "Jealous you never did what we just did!"

The furious mews and cries from the tigermite pack ... very clearly Amber and Scarlet had hit a nerve. A very painful nerve. Seduce and slash was a horrible tradition, and plenty of the beastmite girls mist hate it, but change it? Not within their power.

Blizzard chuckled even more sinisterly in that corner of the tavern.

"Kill those two tigermite traitors," he said, "but leave the boy and his spellblade to me!"

More and more mews and snarls from above. From among the beams and shadows in the ceiling.

Snow tsked. "Mavs, less talkie talkie and more fightie fightie!"

Good. Snow was right.

This fight was life and death—and not just for himself and his newfound girlfriends.

So Maverick raised his spellblade high up and rearing to go.

"Snow," Maverick said, "you know what to do, right?"

"Right!" Snow said.

A crack from the loudest, the brightest, the most powerful bolt of bright-blue lightning split through the room. Forked fast above him. Smelling of fresh winter. Of fresh snow.

Not of metallic anything? Strange but ... ice-natured lightning then.

The ice-natured lightning forked everywhere around the ceiling. All from out of Snow the Spellblade.

Striking at least seven, if not a dozen or so different spots scattered about the ceiling.

But at the same instant another bolt of blue lightning struck.

Matching each and every spot.

"Daring to kill my harem of lovelies?" Blizzard said. "Now yours dies before you!"

A second bolt of lightning—of scarlet red lightning, Fiery lightning smelling of roasted cherries? What the ...

From the other spellblade Blizzard wielded. The scarlet spellblade.

That lightning forked right at Amber and Scarlet.

All while Maverick and his own bright-blue lightning from Snow was held, latched in place at those other spots.

But that very same instant. Both Amber and Scarlet. They screamed out strange words in a lyrical chant. As lyrical as any elf girl's song. A chant that tingled his spine to its core.

A magical chant!

An instant later. Just in time.

All three of them. Maverick. Amber. Scarlet. A half-bubble of amber and scarlet pentagrams surrounded them. Pentagrams of glowing light. Each a few inches big. As big as their pawish hands. They swirled around the three of them. Only paces away.

The lighting struck the bubble-shaped shield of pentagrams.

And both shattered. Shattered into colorful sparks.

Smelling of cherries and peaches? The elven scents Peaches and Cherry were named after? That—

A dozen mews erupted from the shadows all around Maverick, Amber, and Scarlet.

Erupted from the ground around them.

CHAPTER 9
BLIZZARD CLAWSTORM

Blizzard chuckled. Everything was going to plan now —mostly.

The prey now squirmed against the walls of this building out of meager pathetic hope. Hope their future wasn't as dark as this tavern. That the stink of blood and worse wasn't in their future like it was in the building beside them.

Especially the near-naked elf girls.

Smelling so tasty that ... Blizzard gulped. A feast. Very, very soon.

The best kind of feast a wolfmite could hunt for, and feast on.

These puny tables. Long tables and benches. They'll make the hunt easier—not harder. None of the prey could use them to hide—and they blocked straightforward access to any escape.

Escape was impossible—for his pack of tigermite mates would strike any and all down from the shadows.

Strike down any prey who dared try leaving this tavern alive.

Spellblade Pearl already blocked anything her twin sister of a spellblade, Spellblade Snow, threw at Blizzard or anyone else. That boy she dared to spare, that boy couldn't have the stamina to keep using his new spellblade.

Spellblades quickly drained their users stamina—without proper training, that was.

And free spellblades—even more stamina. The price for weakness.

Spellblade Rosaline would soon shattered all other defenses and attacks. Wear down both tigermite traitors. Until Spellblade Rosaline spelled their doom.

If his pack of tigermite mates didn't strike those traitors both down first.

Amber and Scarlet. Their Razorine was pathetic. Predictable to the extreme. As sloppy as any pathetic kitten's. They only trained some of their magic. Fiery magic enhancing their paws and claws, but nothing more.

Nothing to fear. Not without proper training they'd never prove a threat. Ever.

Nothing to worry about.

Any other witch or wizard trapped in here knew better than to reveal themselves yet.

But certainly a few of the prey could fight back—at the right moment.

If the moment ever arrived—and it wouldn't.

Ever.

Spellblade Rosaline now glowed bright and fiercely. Able to blast through any spell any witch or wizard here could toss at them.

Just like Spellblade Pearl.

The only light here now. From the three spellblades and nothing much more.

Not enough to interfere with shadowjumping.

To grant an escape to those tigermite traitors, maybe, if they fled rather than die with their target. The target they dared to spare, to grow fond of and even, as awfully disgusting as it sounded, grew lustful loving toward.

Those two bolts of blue lightning still forked and crackled and screamed around the ceiling. The beams there. At spots his tigermite mates already left.

Blizzard chuckled. Victory was within his claws.

Even as that boy foolish forced himself forward. Clearly eager to get closer and closer to Blizzard. Within striking range of his pathetic Spellblade Snow.

And far within range of Blizzard's own Razorine strikes.

Soon that boy would die. Nothing could save him now.

Snow would soon be bound as a proper spellblade. A twin blade of Spellblade Pearl.

And those two tigermite traitors dead.

"Go get them, girls," Blizzard said. "Feast on their flesh and bones!"

CHAPTER 10
MAVERICK DE MAYHEM

Despite the fierce crackles of the blue bolts of lightning clashing, lightning bolts pinning each other down, flashing blindingly bright light here and there.

Despite the mews, snarls, and cries of Amber, of Scarlet against that pack of tigermite terrors. Their paws and claws raging with flame the color of their name. Combining Razorine martial arts with such fiery magic they obviously learned at Witchengal. Magic keeping that pack of regular tigermite at bay.

For now.

Enough that Maverick marched slowly but steadily toward Blizzard. Toward his two wolfmite buddies. Playing the defiant human for now. The determined hero-to-be.

No obvious plan in sight.

The energy to keep the bolt of lightning going and going.

Maverick could only manage it a few more moments. And that was with Snow doing all the work. Him. Merely the only source of energy, only.

The smell of icy snow. Of winter freshly arriving.

Ice-natured lightning. From both spellblades.

Identical spellblades.

A twin sister.

Maverick. A few steps away from the big brawny Blizzard.

The bolts of lightning cackled even more fiercely between them. Revealing the sinister wolf-snouted face of that wolfmite monster, Blizzard. Revealing the strain, the lose of stamina that Blizzard himself clearly didn't notice.

Yet.

So Maverick gasped.

Bang!

Fell to a knee. His right knee. Against the hard plank floor.

No mercy to his knee.

Just like no beastmite enemy here would show a shred of mercy to the innocent party-goers if Maverick and his girl-friends didn't win the day. The screams and cries from the building next door.

Soon would come from this building. Unless Mavericks turned the situation around.

And quickly.

Now. Blizzard gave Maverick a wicked cackle.

"Tired already?" Blizzard said. "Properly bound spell-blades don't take nearly as much strength to wield. Sparing Snow her freedom will prove your death. And her enslave-ment! By me!"

And Blizzard swung the blade down. Around.

Smashing Snow the Spellblade out of Maverick's hand.

Spellblade flying away.

Crashing onto the floor several steps away. Sliding even further away.

So no hope to survive—had Maverick merely been human.

"Now you die," Blizzard said. "No mercy to the wickedly weak humans. None!"

Maverick grimaced. "Really? Whoever said I was merely human?"

And Maverick lunged. Shifting to his black-furred wolfmite form. Just like he practiced so often with his dad. Dark claws out and ready to slash. Newfound snout full of fangs roaring for blood.

Beastmite blood.

Especially Blizzard's.

And Blizzard. His buddies.

Too shocked to react. React in time.

An instant later. Both buddies. Dead. Split from head to waist.

All thanks to the Razorine skill of throwing arcs of claws. Arcs even sharper. More powerful than a mere strike with those claws.

And Blizzard. No longer a bright white fool of a monster. No. Now he bleed from so many wounds. A bloody mess. A bloody snarling mess.

Unarmed now like Maverick.

His own spellblades gone. Steps away. Somewhere.

"Time for the real battle," Maverick said, "of fang and claw!"

Except a bolt of blue lightning struck Blizzard in the chest. Freezing the entire wolfmite into steamingly chilled ice within moments. Eyes wide in shock. Eyes clouding over in death.

No mews or snarls or cries to avenge their beloved Blizzard from any tigermite.

No.

Those icy crackles. Coming not just from Blizzard—but from over a dozen spots throughout the tavern.

Nothing from next door either—except cheers of victory?

Snow tsked right behind Maverick. "One fling and forgotten already ..."

"Snow, I ..." Maverick said, turning around, but not shifting back.

Not yet.

So Snow hugged her beloved lunk of wolf boy. No chance to escape her cuddly hug this time—or ever again.

And Maverick. He hugged her back.

Just as relieved—and her scent now. Woh.

As amazingly wonderfully foxy fun as the rest of her now.

CHAPTER II
MAVERICK DE MAYHEM

Moments, if not minutes later it all was but certain the festival was over, least for the time being.

No party-goers were hurt here—fortunately, but elsewhere ... more than certainly so.

Least the storm started easing up. Less thunder. Less lightning. All further away.

Rain easing up to a light drizzle. Pickering and patters everywhere outside. Wind dying down and fading. Just like the storm itself.

As if the storm had been powered by a now-dead monster mage.

Murmurs came from the party-goers still crowded by the walls. Nervous but not hateful toward any of their beastmite savors.

Even when the front door swung open. His dad standing there.

In full black-furred wolfmite form.

Maverick could only stare at his big brawny dad as he lugged the corpse of a big black-furred ratling over his broad shoulders.

Let out the loudest barrel of a laugh despite the dim light.

"Some very good bounties here too," dad said. "Maverick, save those two spellblades for Nat. He'll free the foxmites trapped inside—unless some lovely witches here at Witchengal will do it—"

"Of course!"

From several of the scantily clad elf girls.

Right then and there all those scantily clad elf girls actually volunteered to work together to free the foxmites trapped within the spellblades.

Soon, in back, within the corner opposite of the three dead wolfmites, the whole lot of elven witches were busy at work.

Drake waited back there too. No words between Maverick and Drake—a reassured glance. That was all they needed.

Before Drake resumed staring intently at that scarlet-red spellblade.

All while Snow stared intent and worried at the blue spellblade. Maverick side-hugging his dear newfound mate. Just like Amber and Scarlet comforting Snow from the other side. Their purrs and whispers. Genuinely worried as well.

But within minutes two more foxmites were among that crowd of elf witches.

Even in the dim light there was no missing how much one of the two foxmites practically glowed with white fur. That white-furred beauty looked exactly like Snow—down to the fur strand. Same long blonde hair. Same blue eyes. Same everything

Except actually completely bare in the fur, and clearly not minding it.

More like enjoying it—especially when Snow jumped in and hugged her.

Tugging her beloved Maverick along for the ride.

Their giggles. Worth all the trouble in the world.

Especially when Amber and Scarlet joined them too.

Just like the hugs and giggles between Drake and woh, that scarlet foxmite was as beautiful as Snow and that newly freed twin sister of hers.

A breath of her foxy scent and yeah, another sister of Snow's.

Good for Drake. At this rate they'd end up not just brothers-im-arms, but brothers-in-laws.

That's when dad howled for everyone's attention. Still standing in the broken doorway. The drizzle behind him all but stopped. The street looked more like a canal than a street but with those currents no swimming—least for now.

With another barrel of a laugh, and a pair of grateful gorgeous girls of the scantily clad kind beside him and in his arms already, dad announced the obvious.

"Now for the victory party!" dad said, "Food and drink all on me!"

The crowd cheered. The fiddlers started fiddling once again.

And the festival party when on and on.

ABOUT THE AUTHOR

Widely traveled, Jonathan Evan Hudson spends as much time studying life as he does writing gripping tales of fantastic adventures. From the giant redwoods of California to the deserts of Israel, his thrilling stories all draw on first-hand experiences and expand them with the fantastic and his acclaimed creativity.

Be the first to know!
For the updates and more:
www.JonathanEvanHudson.com

youtube.com/@jonathanevanhudson
tiktok.com/@jonathan.evan.hudson

A War Of Lust And Oak

Read Now!

The Elf Girl Effect

Read Now!

The acclaimed Jonathan Evan Hudson once again weaves an unforgettable tale brimming with spicy page-turning action and fast-burning enemies-to-lovers passion.

Meet the newly knighted Roo Vorshaya. Sworn to protect humanity in the isolated mountain town of Appleharth. Dreams of action-packed adventure and passionate love under a lovely but sinister strawberry-pink sky.

Love re-ignited by a whiff of the familiar peaches and cream scent of his long-lost childhood girlfriend: the notorious elven witch Amber Peaches.

And endangering everything Roo holds dear.

Love page-turner novels of epic fantasy? Love reading from dusk to dawn? Then go read *The Elf Girl Effect* now!

Martial Art Of The Phantom Saber

Read Now!

Succubus Slash

Read Now!

The acclaimed Jonathan Evan Hudson weaves an unforgettable tale of thrilling action and adventure spiced with fast-burning romance and doused deep in epic fantasy.

Enter Miles Mayhem. Rich in friends and enemies. And a fat boy badass in the sword.

A seriously delicious smell of bacon and eggs smothered in spiced razor-hot cheddar signals celebration—and serious trouble ahead.

Trouble beyond anything Miles ever expected.

The perfect epic fantasy novel. A genre-enlarging feast for fans of sexy action and fabulous adventure. Read *Succubus Slash* now!

Into Shadow Forest

Read Now!

A diamond in the rough the bestselling Jonathan Evan Hudson weaves a thrilling tale from explosive beginning to satisfying end in the awe-inspiring land of Grandcrest.

The talented twenty-something sword master Romeo Bladell yearns for love and adventure.

And at the musty edges of Shadow Forest. Near the towering high oaks bearded like stout old dwarves. By a canyon like a wound gnashed deep through in the granite. A canyon like the maw of a stone dragon.

A strange unexpected rope bridge hangs silently. Sinisterly.

Beckoning adventure—and danger unimaginable.

Enter *Into Shadow Forest* and savor the most spectacular of page-turning epic fantasy novels. Love unique monsters, riveting battles, and fantastic femme fatales? Then read *Into Shadow Forest* now!

Angels Of The Sword

Read Now!

CROSSING OF SHADOWED DEATH

The acclaimed master of fantasy Jonathan Evan Hudson once again shines through with his talented story-telling. Time to enter another stunning awe-inspiring world of dangerous demons, magical mayhem, and action-packed adventure.

A simple demon-hunting mission. The young and lonely Dirk yearns for amazing adventure, for gorgeously under-dressed dancer girls among the towering high ferns. Among the even taller pines of the hot and humid Fern Shadow Forest.

Pine needles everywhere. And so fragrant they made the finest of teas.

Sturdy reliable cobble roads of the Divine Empire cut through the whole entire forest. Providing the only safe passage.

Or so Dirk thought ...

Enjoy this sexy, action-packed epic fantasy adventure from the talented Jonathan Evan Hudson. Love to read an enthralling epic fantasy novel full of stunning rip-roaring battles with creative new monsters? Then go read *Crossing of Shadowed Death* now!

A TASTE OF CROSSING OF SHADOWED DEATH

The acclaimed master of fantasy Jonathan Evan Hudson once again shines through with his talented story-telling. Time to enter another stunning awe-inspiring world of dangerous demons, magical mayhem, and action-packed adventure.

A simple demon-hunting mission. The young and lonely Dirk yearns for amazing adventure, for gorgeously under-dressed dancer girls among the towering high ferns. Among the even taller pines of the hot and humid Fern Shadow Forest.

Pine needles everywhere. And so fragrant they made the finest of teas.

Sturdy reliable cobble roads of the Divine Empire cut through the whole entire forest. Providing the only safe passage.

Or so Dirk thought ...

Enjoy this sexy, action-packed epic fantasy adventure from the talented Jonathan Evan Hudson. Love to read an enthralling epic fantasy novel full of stunning rip-roaring battles with creative new monsters? Then go read **Crossing of Shadowed Death** *now!*

CHAPTER 1
DIRK

The mission was simple, really.

Just deliver a message to the mayor of a town called Grassbarn. Exterminate some demons known as Tentacled Shrooms and Chicken Nixies roaming the nearby farmers' fields. Before they attack some any poor human that crossed their path and eat their soul.

Maybe even turn them to zombies.

Now Tentacled Shrooms were the size of big dogs and looked exactly like they sounded, at least according to the mission statement. Same for Chicken Nixies. Some kind of cross between chicken and snake.

Simple but thrilling.

Nothing too troublesome, but work that needed to be done.

And only an Angel of the Sword could do it.

Only they would wield the divine silver that could slash through any demons and its powers and so on and so forth.

And divine silver came from the Divinity of the Heavenlies within those people Chosen by the Heavenlies, so no matter rank or station, only those with a Divinity could ever hope to become Angels of the Sword.

(More like had to but ...)

Lots of travel opportunities. Travel the world. Paid for by the Palace of the Heavenlies, so quite the Blessing right there, getting to see things only Angels of the Sword could hope to go see.

Like Fern Shadow Forest.

Where the ferns were so big many of them were far higher than the average horse. Even beside the cobble roads that ran everywhere throughout the Divine Empire, including Fern Shadow Forest. Their leaves were so big and long ... especially if you were down laying on the ground, they were titan-sized ferns.

No wonder the famously beautiful dancer girls of Fern Shadow Forest were famous throughout the lands for their elaborate fern slutwear.

(And they were certainly a Blessing of the Heavenlies.)

(Even if a certain grandmother would disagree. Vehemently, as she'd say.)

And these parts were so hot that it was like being stuffed inside a barrel and left on the docks again.

So the dancer girls shouldn't be blamed for under-dressing.

Rumor even had it they had some intriguing combat techniques too, even if rumors were often just rumors.

And here in Fern Shadow Forest, a chance to find out.

Pine needles beautifully mattressed the ground everywhere off the cobble road. Like an orange carpet. With wonderful pine aroma. Especially around the huuuge crooked pines. Pines called pitched pines, it turned out.

And these pines even had incredibly spooky faces. Each and every one of them.

Above the ferns.

The pine needles made a tea that couldn't be made elsewhere. Apparently, unlike other conifers, these needles must of freshly turned orange or else the tea wouldn't be any good.

All in all, an adventure worth having and not much trouble until ... well ...

CHAPTER 2
DIRK

Flat on his back as if he fell off another Heavenlies-cursed horse again, Dirk stared up at the wide expanse of clear blue sky and thanked the Heavenlies it wouldn't be his last.

(Also thank the Heavenlies there was no Hell-worthy beast known as a horse involved this time.)

(Really thankful.)

The rock here was as smooth and bumpy as the fat landlord's knuckles against his chin for missing rent once again, and actually ...

That was a month ago.

Already ...

But a few bruises for a few more days were worth it, of course, whether it was bruises on his chin or his back, they built character, as Grandmother Tressia would say.

She also insisted he savor the blessings in life.

Like ... how the branch that (somehow) flung him flat onto his back was nowhere in sight, so it must of suffered a far worse fate than him.

The solid rock beneath him, just another reminder to be thankful. Like it not being his shallow new grave. Much like how that poor old fox almost met the wrong end of a speeding wagon in the last village, what's its name, Briarton, I think.

Except Dirk chucked a rock at the right moment.

And he got a knuckle sandwich from an irritated wagoner in return.

But Angels help those in need.

Unless they be demons then ... (maybe?)

And landing here, on his back, a real blessing.

A good few more feet back and that loud trinkle left no doubt, he'd be underwater.

In the stream called the Mateedoh-Klonk River.

Its dark water had many trinkling bumps, all incredibly smooth. Not a single sign of a single bubble or hint of foam.

Or of any rock.

The stream was so small a simple hop was enough to cross it, but today, it was so hot, it was like being stuffed inside a barrel and left on the docks again. So a dip in cool water was, of course, tempting.

Only minutes before, Dirk had stuck a long branch under those waters and yank!

So quick the branch was ripped out of his hand.

It was so deep and rough, if you got sucked in, you'd never resurface, ever.

No hope of swimming 'cross that water.

Even if it smelled like the best kind of pine needle tea, it was too dangerous to try drinking from. How many poor travelers had died trying to fill their water flasks with it?

Must be too many to count and probably the reason the main road looped so long and hard to avoid this side road, but no, Dirk didn't have the time to waste and a little sense went a far way.

Sure, that hollow echo of water under a bridge, that was from a small arch of stone that served to bridge the stream, as expected of anywhere in the Divine Empire, just like how the bridge and the cobble road were still intact.

This bridge even had railings, unlike most of the small arch bridges scattered around the empire. The fact this bridge was stone rather than solid oak, another sign that this stream was more dangerous than it first appeared. It wasn't unheard of for wood bridges to rot enough for a collapse this far out of the way.

Of course, Dirk knew better than to ever trust a stray bridge.

He had leapt across the stream.

It was small enough, and the bridge ... it could be a mimic.

Gulp.

And mimics took the place an inanimate object, somehow, and the moment a victim used it, it would swallow the poor victim – or victims – whole.

Then vanish.

Nothing remaining.

No sign of what happened remained – except the missing inanimate object

But mimics wouldn't – or couldn't – pose as cups or small objects (thank the Heavenlies) or objects that were too big (really thank the Heavenlies), but … if he hadn't seen it first-hand … back when he was so young … then maybe bridges … no.

The Heavenlies-cursed horse he had been on panicked … nearly tossed him onto the bridge mimic – the damn cowardly beast and … the scars on his feet, across his shins hurt just from thinking of it …

Since even bigger bridge than the one over the Mateedoh-Klonk River had turned out to be a mimic and gulped a bunch of victims and then shrunk and vanished …

Only to reappear elsewhere somehow … where there hadn't been a bridge moments before … trapping him on that … that …

WANT MORE?

Go to

WANT MORE?

Go to

www.JonathanEvanHudson.com

www.ingramcontent.com/pod-product-compliance
Lightning Source LLC
Chambersburg PA
CBHW030821200726
48288CB00004B/1334